A CUP OF TEA WE NEVER FINISHED

TROUGH THE ASHES OF PAHALGAM

MANDA SAHITHI SREE

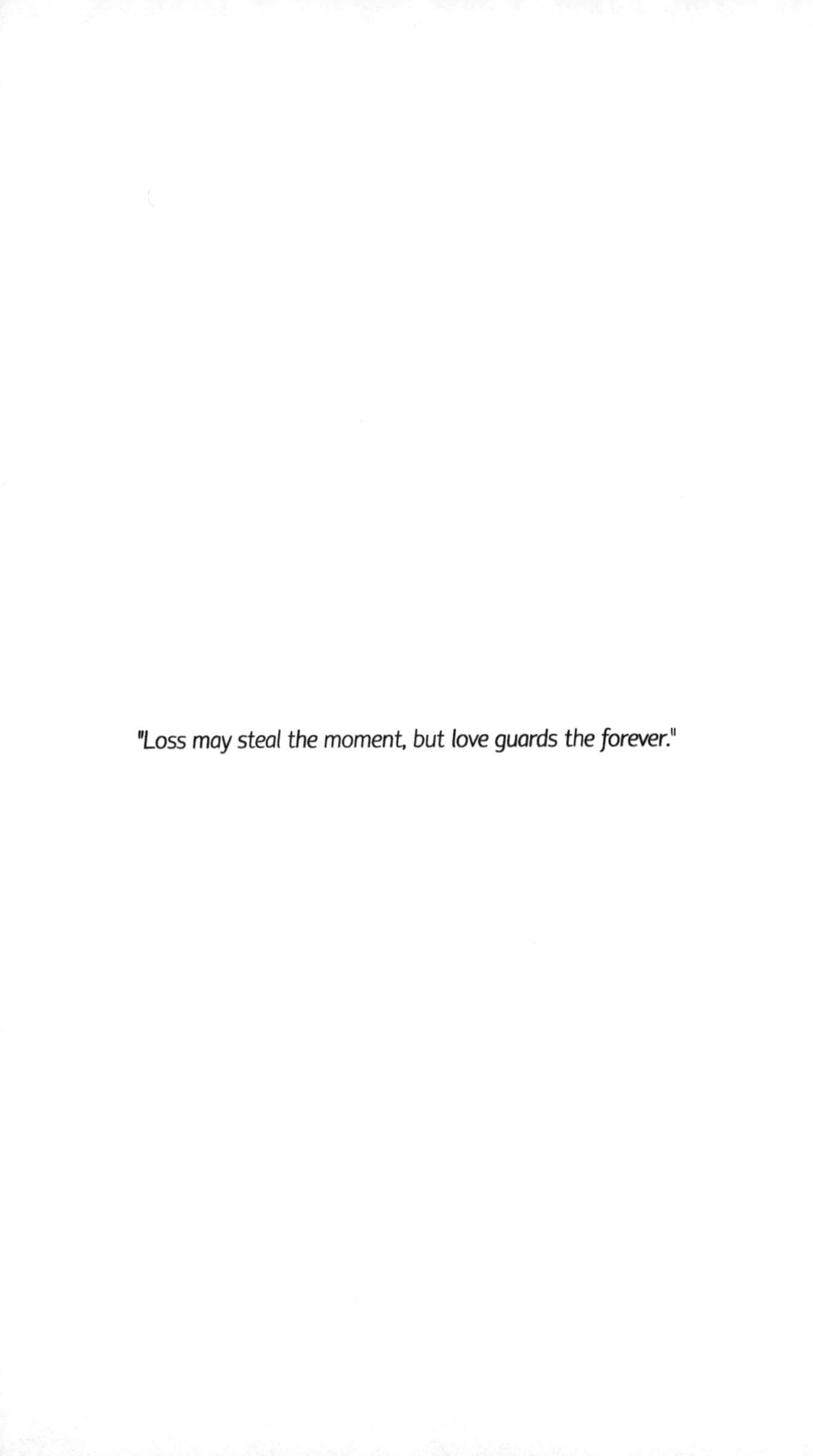

"Loss may steal the moment, but love guards the forever."

Contents

Foreword

This book was written from the heart — for every person who has loved deeply, lost suddenly, and still found the strength to move forward.

"A Cup of Tea We Never Finished" is a story of two sisters whose world changes in an instant. It's about the pain of goodbye, the strength of love, and the hope that slowly returns with time.

I hope this story stays with you, not just as a tale of tragedy, but as a reminder of courage, family, and the power of holding on to each other.

With my heart,
Sahithi Sree

Preface

This story began with a simple thought: how quickly life can change, and how deeply love can endure.

"A Cup of Tea We Never Finished" is not just a tale of tragedy. It is a journey through love, loss, and the strength that rises from the ruins. Sneha's story may be fictional, but her emotions are real, drawn from the quiet pain many feel, yet often leave unspoken.

As the author, I wrote this book with a heart full of empathy and hope. It is a tribute to families torn apart too soon, to sisters who find each other in the dark, and to anyone who has had to grow stronger before they were ready.

This book is for the brave.

This book is for you.

With my heart,

Sahithi Sree

Acknowledgements

To you, dear reader, thank you for picking up this book and letting this story touch your heart. Your time means everything.

To Sneha, for your strength, love, and courage. You are the heart of this story.

To her parents, your love lives on, even in silence.

To Aanya, for your innocence, your growth, and the quiet hope you carry.

To my parents and my sister, thank you for believing in me, giving me strength, and encouraging me to write this book.

To Sathwika, for your constant support, honest advice, and for gently guiding this book into its better version. I'm so grateful for your presence through every chapter.

And to myself, for not giving up, for working hard, and for turning emotions into something meaningful.

With all my heart,
Sahithi Sree

Prologue

Sneha- Their Little World

Before the snow, before the silence, there was laughter.

There was Sneha, a 19-year-old, bright-eyed and full of dreams. And there was her world: a world not made of riches, but of warmth. A family stitched together by care, laughter, and small, everyday magic.

Sneha's father, Rajesh, was a government employee. Quiet, principled, and the kind of man who'd put an extra biscuit on her plate without saying a word. Her mother, Meera, ran a home filled with light. She had a hundred stories in her eyes and a way of making every cup of tea taste like peace. And then there was Aanya — the giggling whirlwind, 11 and full of spark, who followed Sneha around like a second shadow.

Their home was small but alive — with music, shared meals, late-night board games, and debates about which movie to watch. Every Sunday, without fail, they'd sit together on the balcony for chai and pakoras. It wasn't just a snack — it was a sacred ritual. Laughter would bounce between the walls, Aanya teasing Sneha about her singing, their father quoting old Hindi poets, their mother reminding them to cherish every moment.

In those little corners of life, they found their heaven.

On the day before the Kashmir trip, Meera said something over tea. She smiled, her fingers warm around her cup, and said,

"Promise me, girls — no quarreling this time. Be kind to each other. That's what matters, always."*

Sneha had rolled her eyes but smiled, tugging Aanya's braid playfully.

"I'll try. But no promises with this monkey around."

They had all laughed. Loud, full laughter — the kind you never imagine will end.

That was their last evening at home.

"our Little World"

Poem from Sneha's journal "Our Little World"
*We didn't have much, just love and tea,
A little world — just Aanya, them, and me.
Laughter lived in every room,
And warm hugs chased away all gloom.
Now it's quieter, not the same,
But their love still whispers my name.
Our world may have changed, it's true,
But in my heart, it lives anew.*

CHAPTER ONE

The Dream Vacation

The sun peeked over the horizon, casting a warm golden glow across the lush green valleys of Pahalgam. The air was crisp and fresh, filled with the scent of pine and the promise of adventure. Sneha and Aanya sat in the backseat of their family car, their excitement bubbling over as they drove towards their favorite getaway. This was more than just a trip; it was a cherished family tradition that brought them closer together.

"Are we there yet?" Aanya chirped, her voice filled with anticipation. Her wide eyes sparkled with eagerness as she peered out the window, watching the landscape transform from bustling city streets to serene mountain roads.

"Just a little longer, champ!" their father, Rajesh, replied with a chuckle, glancing back at his daughters through the rearview mirror. "Remember, the best adventures take time to reach!"

Their mother, Meera, smiled as she adjusted the playlist on the car's stereo. "How about we listen to your favorite songs while we drive? Let's make some memories!"

As the familiar tunes filled the car, Sneha and Aanya began to sing along, their voices harmonizing in joyful unison. They laughed and danced in their seats, the worries of the world fading away with each note. The bond they shared as sisters was evident in every laugh, every playful nudge, and every shared secret.

When they finally arrived at Pahalgam, the sight took their breath away. The verdant mountains stood tall against the azure sky, and the sound of the flowing river filled the air with a soothing melody. Sneha, the older sister at twelve, felt a sense of responsibility wash over her as she looked after her younger sister, Aanya, who was just eight.

"Look at that river!" Aanya exclaimed, her eyes wide with wonder. "Can we go swimming right now?"

"Of course! But let's set up our things first," Meera suggested, guiding them to unload the car. The family quickly set up their picnic area by the riverbank, laying out colorful blankets and unpacking baskets filled with delicious homemade treats.

Once everything was ready, the girls wasted no time. They raced towards the river, laughter echoing as they splashed into the cool water. Sneha dove in first, her heart racing with exhilaration as she swam out a few meters, feeling the refreshing rush of the current against her skin.

"Come on, Aanya! The water is amazing!" Sneha called, her voice filled with joy. Aanya hesitated for a moment, then took a deep breath and jumped in, her squeals of delight mingling with the sound of the rushing water.

The girls spent hours in the river, playing games, splashing each other, and floating on their backs while they watched the fluffy clouds drift lazily across the sky. Sneha taught Aanya how to do a backstroke, her laughter ringing out as Aanya flailed her arms and legs, trying to keep up.

"Just like this!" Sneha demonstrated, gliding effortlessly through the water. Aanya watched intently, her determination shining through. "I can do it, Sneha! I can!" she shouted, her enthusiasm infectious.

After a while, they took a break, lounging on the sun-warmed rocks by the riverbank. Their parents joined them, sharing sandwiches and fruit, and the family laughed as they recounted funny stories from past trips.

"Remember the time we got lost on the hiking trail?" Rajesh asked, his eyes twinkling with mischief. "You two were convinced we'd never find our way back!"

"Dad, you were the one with the map!" Sneha teased, nudging Aanya playfully. "But we did find our way back, didn't we?"

"Thanks to Mom's sense of direction!" Aanya chimed in, giggling.

Meera smiled, her heart swelling with love for her family. "And the snacks I packed! Never underestimate the power of snacks!"

After their delightful picnic, the family decided to try something new: water skiing. Rajesh had rented a couple of surfboards, and the girls could hardly contain their excitement. "This is going to be epic!" Aanya squealed, her eyes shining with anticipation.

Sneha felt a mix of thrill and nervousness. She had never surfed before, but she was determined to show Aanya that they could conquer anything together. "Let's do this!" she declared, her resolve firm.

They waded into the water, boards in hand. Rajesh demonstrated how to balance and ride the waves, his confidence inspiring the girls. "Just remember to keep your knees bent and your eyes on the horizon," he instructed, his voice steady.

One by one, they took their turns. Sneha watched Aanya catch her first wave, her little sister's face lighting up with pure joy as she rode it all the way to the shore. "I did it! I did it!" Aanya shouted, her laughter ringing like music in the air.

Sneha's heart swelled with pride. "You were amazing, Aanya!" she cheered, clapping her hands.

Now it was Sneha's turn. She took a deep breath, feeling the rush of adrenaline as she paddled out. The waves crashed around her, and for a moment, she felt a surge of fear. But then she remembered Aanya's excitement and her parents cheering from the shore. With renewed determination, she focused on the horizon, finding her balance as she stood up on the board.

"Go, Sneha!" Aanya shouted, her voice filled with encouragement.

As she caught a wave, the thrill of riding it surged through her. Sneha felt invincible, the wind whipping through her hair and the water splashing around her. She laughed out loud, the sound echoing across the water as she glided toward the shore, exhilarated.

When she finally fell off the board, she surfaced to see Aanya and their parents clapping and cheering. "That was incredible!" Meera called, her face alight with pride.

After several rounds of surfing, they returned to the shore, breathless and happy. The sun began to set, painting the sky in hues of orange and pink. The family gathered around a small campfire, roasting marshmallows and sharing stories under the vast expanse of stars.

"Look at the stars!" Aanya exclaimed, her eyes wide with wonder. "It's like they're twinkling just for us!"

Sneha wrapped her arm around her sister, pulling her close. "They are, Aanya. Just like our memories will always shine bright in our hearts."

As they sat together, sharing laughter and love, Sneha felt a deep sense of gratitude wash over her. This was what life was about—these moments of pure joy, the bonds of family, and the memories they created together. She looked at her parents, their faces illuminated by the firelight, and felt a warmth in her heart.

"Promise me we'll always have adventures like this," Aanya said, her voice soft but filled with sincerity.

"I promise," Sneha replied, her heart swelling with love. "No matter what happens, we'll always be together, creating memories and living life to the fullest."

And in that moment, surrounded by the warmth of family and the beauty of nature, Sneha knew that this day would forever be etched in their hearts—a day filled with laughter, love, and the unbreakable bond that tied them all together.

CHAPTER TWO

The Unthinkable

The third day of their vacation dawned bright and beautiful, the sun casting a golden hue over the snow-capped mountains. Sneha awoke with a flutter of excitement, her heart brimming with the promise of adventure. After a hearty breakfast, they set out for a hike through the higher mountains, the crisp air invigorating their spirits.

As they walked, the world around them felt enchanted. Aanya's laughter rang like music, filling the air with joy. Sneha couldn't help but smile at her sister's exuberance, her heart swelling with love. They ventured further into the mountains, away from the bustling tourist spots, seeking the untouched beauty of Kashmir. The path was quiet, flanked by towering trees that whispered secrets in the wind. Villagers waved at them, their friendly smiles a stark contrast to the unsettling feeling that began to creep into Sneha's heart.

But as they climbed higher, the atmosphere shifted. The once cheerful chirping of birds faded into an eerie silence. Sneha noticed the locals exchanging worried glances, their faces drawn tight with unspoken fear. Her father, always attuned to the world around him, grew quiet, his brow furrowing with concern. "Let's head back," he suggested, his voice steady but laced with an urgency that sent a chill down Sneha's spine.

Just as they began retracing their steps, a sound shattered the tranquility—a sharp, deafening crack that echoed through the valley. Gunfire. The world around them transformed into chaos, the serene beauty of nature now tainted by terror. Sneha's heart raced as screams pierced the air, frantic and filled with despair.

"Run!" her father shouted, his voice cutting through the panic as he pulled them towards the trees for cover. The ground trembled beneath their feet, and the acrid smell of gunpowder filled the air, choking Sneha as she clutched Aanya's hand, her fingers trembling.

"Stay close!" she urged, fear tightening her throat. They ducked behind a large boulder, Sneha's breath coming in shallow gasps. The world outside felt like a nightmare—screams, shouts, and the relentless barrage of gunfire echoing around them.

During the chaos, Sneha could hear her mother's voice, calling out to her, searching for them. "Sneha! Aanya!" It was a sound that would haunt her forever. "Stay down!" her father cried, his eyes scanning the surroundings with a fierce protectiveness that only a father could possess.

But then, in a split second that felt like an eternity, the chaos erupted into silence. The gunfire ceased, and the screams faded into an unbearable quiet. Sneha dared to look around, her heart pounding in her chest. "Mom? Dad?" she called out, her voice trembling. Panic surged through her as she realized—her parents were gone.

"Where are they?" Aanya whimpered, her innocent eyes wide with fear and confusion. Sneha pulled her sister closer, her heart breaking as she felt the weight of their reality crashing down on her. They were alone now. Alone in a foreign land, surrounded by strangers, with no one left to turn to.

The silence that followed was suffocating. Sneha's mind raced, grappling with the horror of the moment. They had come to Kashmir for a dream vacation, a time to bond and create memories. Instead, they were thrust into a nightmare that shattered their world.

Days turned into a blur of confusion and grief. Sneha and Aanya wandered through the remnants of the town, lost and scared, the echoes of that day haunting their every step. The authorities were overwhelmed, and the survivors were struggling to find safety amidst the chaos. They had no relatives in Kashmir, no one to guide them, no one to comfort them in their grief.

Every night, they huddled together in their makeshift shelter, trying to find solace in each other's presence. Aanya, too young to fully grasp the enormity of what had happened, clung to Sneha, her wide eyes constantly searching for their parents. "When will they come back?" she would ask, her voice small and fragile, filled with a hope that felt painfully misplaced.

Sneha would stroke Aanya's hair, fighting back tears. "Soon, Aanya. They'll come back soon." But deep down, she knew the truth. The cruel reality of loss was something she had never prepared for.

Then, just as despair threatened to consume them, a glimmer of hope appeared in the form of the Indian Army. Soldiers arrived, their presence a beacon of safety amidst the turmoil. They worked tirelessly to evacuate the survivors, providing comfort and reassurance. Sneha and Aanya were taken under the protective wing of the soldiers, their hearts heavy with the weight of what they had lost.

As they were led away from the chaos, the sisters looked back at the town, now shrouded in shadows. Sneha's heart ached with a profound sadness. "Will we ever go back?" she whispered to Aanya, her voice trembling.

Aanya's eyes filled with tears. "I want Mom and Dad," she cried, the innocence of her words piercing through Sneha's heart like a dagger. In that moment, the reality of their loss hit her with full force. They were being taken home, but home would never be the same again.

The journey back was surreal. Surrounded by soldiers, Sneha felt a flicker of safety, but it was overshadowed by the gnawing emptiness in her heart. As they arrived at the army base, the reality of their situation settled in. They were safe, but their parents were gone, leaving behind a void that felt insurmountable.

In the quiet of the night, as they lay in their temporary shelter, Sneha finally allowed herself to break down. She wept for her parents, for the life they had lost, for the dreams that would never be realized. Aanya curled up beside her, her small body shaking with silent sobs. "I miss them, Sneha," she whispered, her voice laced with sorrow.

"I miss them too," Sneha choked out, wrapping her arms around her sister, holding her tightly as if to shield her from the pain. "But we have each other. We'll get through this together."

And in that moment, as tears streamed down her face, Sneha made a silent promise to her parents—to honor their love, their teachings, and to protect Aanya with every ounce of strength she had left. They would find a way to carry on, even if the road ahead seemed impossibly dark.

CHAPTER THREE

Alone In The World

The silence that enveloped Sneha and Aanya in the aftermath of the attack was deafening, a haunting reminder of the chaos they had just escaped. The Indian Army had brought them to a temporary shelter, a place that felt both safe and suffocating. Despite the presence of soldiers, the shadows of fear and grief loomed large, casting a pall over their fragile existence.

In the days that followed, the sisters found themselves caught in a whirlwind of confusion and despair. The world outside their shelter buzzed with activity as soldiers worked tirelessly to restore order, but inside, time seemed to stand still. Each day felt like a haunting echo of the last, filled with the same unbearable weight of loss.

Sneha struggled to process the reality of their situation. Her parents—her anchors in a stormy sea—were gone. The cruel finality of it all left her feeling adrift, lost in a world that had suddenly turned upside down. Aanya, too young to fully understand the enormity of their loss, wandered through her days with wide, searching eyes, often clutching a small stuffed bear that had once belonged to their mother.

"Why can't we go home?" Aanya would ask, her voice trembling with confusion. "When will Mom and Dad come back?" Each question cut through Sneha like a knife, the innocence of her sister's words a painful reminder of the reality they faced.

Sneha would hold Aanya close, her heart breaking anew each time. "I don't know, Aanya. I wish I could tell you. I wish I could bring them back." Tears would spill down her cheeks, and she would wipe them away quickly, not wanting to show Aanya how much she was hurting. But the truth was, she was terrified. Terrified of the unknown, terrified of being the one to keep them both afloat.

At night, when the world outside grew quiet, Sneha would lie awake, her heart heavy with sorrow. The darkness felt suffocating, and she often found herself staring at the ceiling, replaying memories of her parents in her mind. The sound of her mother's laughter, the warmth of her father's embrace—each memory was a bittersweet reminder of the love that had been so cruelly taken from them.

One evening, as the sun dipped below the horizon, painting the sky in hues of orange and pink, Aanya curled up beside her, her small body trembling. "I'm scared, Sneha," she whispered, her voice barely audible. "What if we never see them again?"

Sneha's heart shattered at her sister's words. The fear in Aanya's eyes was a reflection of her own, a mirror of the anguish that had become their constant companion. "We will see them again, Aanya," she promised, her voice thick with emotion. "In our hearts. They will always be with us."

But deep down, Sneha felt the weight of her promise. How could she reassure Aanya when she herself was struggling to believe those words? She wanted to be strong for her sister, to be the rock that her parents had always been for them. But the truth was, she felt like she was crumbling under the pressure.

As the days turned into weeks, the sisters tried to find some semblance of normalcy amidst the chaos. They were assigned to a temporary home, a small room in a makeshift shelter where other survivors gathered. The walls were thin, and the sounds of grief and sorrow echoed around them, a constant reminder of the loss that had shattered their lives.

Every night, as they lay in their small bed, Aanya would cling to Sneha, seeking comfort in her sister's presence. "Tell me a story, Sneha," she would say, her voice small and fragile. "A happy story."

Sneha would take a deep breath, forcing a smile as she wove tales of adventure and love, stories that once filled their home with laughter. But inside, she was fighting back tears, each story a struggle against the tide of grief that threatened to pull her under. "Once upon a time, there were two brave sisters who went on the greatest adventure of their lives," she would begin, her voice trembling but steady. "They climbed mountains and crossed rivers, and no matter what happened, they always looked out for each other."

Aanya would listen intently, her eyes wide with wonder, and for a brief moment, the weight of their reality would lift. But as soon as the story ended, the silence would return, heavy and suffocating.

One night, as they lay in bed, Aanya suddenly turned to her, her eyes glistening with tears. "Sneha, I don't want to forget them. I don't want to forget Mom and Dad."

The raw pain in her sister's voice pierced through Sneha's heart like a dagger. "You won't forget them, Aanya. We'll keep their memory alive, I promise." But even as she spoke, doubt crept in. How could she ensure that Aanya would remember the warmth of their mother's smile, the strength of their father's embrace, when all they had left were fading memories?

In that moment, Sneha felt the weight of the world on her shoulders. She was not just grieving; she was now responsible for Aanya's happiness, her safety, her very future. The enormity of it all felt crushing.

The following day, as they walked through the camp, they encountered other children playing, their laughter ringing through the air. Aanya's eyes lit up, and she pulled Sneha towards them. "Can we play?" she asked, hope shining in her eyes.

Sneha hesitated, her heart aching. She wanted nothing more than to see her sister smile, but the thought of joining in felt like a betrayal to their parents' memory. "Maybe later," she said softly, her voice barely above a whisper.

But Aanya's face fell, and in that moment, Sneha realized that they needed to find joy again, even amidst the pain. "Okay," she finally relented, forcing a smile. "Let's go play."

As they joined the other children, Sneha felt a flicker of warmth in her heart. She watched Aanya laugh and run, her spirit momentarily lifted. But beneath the surface, the grief still lingered, a shadow that loomed over their every moment.

That night, as they lay in bed, Aanya turned to her, her voice barely above a whisper. "Sneha, do you think Mom and Dad are watching us?"

The question hung in the air, heavy with longing. Sneha swallowed hard, her heart aching. "I believe they are, Aanya. I believe they're always with us, cheering us on."

As tears streamed down her face, she held Aanya close, feeling the warmth of her sister's small body against her own. In that moment, Sneha understood that their parents' love would never truly leave them. It would live on in the stories they shared, in the memories they cherished, and in the bond that had been forged through their shared grief.

And so, as they drifted off to sleep, Sneha whispered a silent prayer to the universe, a plea for strength and guidance. She vowed to honor her parents' memory by nurturing the love that had

brought them together, to keep Aanya safe, and to find a way to navigate the darkness that lay ahead.

Together, they would face whatever came next, one step at a time, holding on to the love that would never fade.

CHAPTER FOUR

After The Silence

The journey back home felt surreal, as if they were walking through a dream that blurred the lines between reality and memory. The familiar streets of their neighborhood greeted them like old friends, but everything felt different. The laughter of children playing, the scent of blooming flowers, and the warmth of the sun on their skin all seemed to mock the heaviness in Sneha's heart.

As they stepped into their house, the silence enveloped them like a shroud. It was a space filled with echoes of laughter, love, and warmth, now haunted by the absence of their parents. Sneha's heart ached as she took in the familiar surroundings—the family photos on the walls, the cozy living room where they had spent countless evenings together, the kitchen that had always been filled with the aroma of her mother's cooking. Each corner of the house held memories that felt both comforting and painful.

Aanya wandered into the living room, her small fingers tracing the edges of a photo frame that held a picture of their family. "I miss them, Sneha," she whispered, her voice trembling. "Will it always be like this?"

Sneha knelt beside her sister, wrapping her arms around her. "I miss them too, Aanya. But we have to be strong. They wouldn't want us to be sad forever." Tears streamed down her face as she spoke, the weight of her promise to her parents pressing heavily on her heart. She had vowed to take care of Aanya, to be the guardian her sister needed in this dark time.

In the days that followed, the reality of their situation began to sink in. They were home, but it felt like a hollow shell of what it once was. Their relatives, sensing the opportunity to seize their parents' assets, began to circle like vultures, eager to offer "help" while eyeing the financial benefits that came with it. Sneha could see the greed in their eyes, the way they calculated the value of their parents' insurance policies and life savings.

"Don't worry, we'll take care of you," one aunt said, her voice dripping with false concern. "You'll need someone to manage the finances. You're just children."

But Sneha felt a fire ignite within her. "I don't need anyone to take care of us," she declared, her voice steady despite the tremor of grief that lingered in her heart. "I can do this. I promised Mom and Dad I would take care of Aanya, and I will. We don't need help from anyone who only wants our money."

Her words hung in the air, a declaration of independence that both frightened and empowered her. She could feel Aanya's eyes on her, wide with admiration and a hint of fear. Sneha knew she had to be strong, not just for herself but for her sister. They would navigate this path together, hand in hand.

As the weeks passed, they began to settle into a new routine. Sneha took on the responsibilities of managing their finances, using the life insurance and savings that their parents had meticulously planned for their education and future. It was a daunting task, but she approached it with determination, fueled by the love and memories of her parents.

Every evening, after Aanya went to bed, Sneha would sit at the kitchen table, poring over the documents, calculating their expenses, and planning for their future. It was during these quiet moments that the weight of her parents' absence felt the heaviest. She would often pause, closing her eyes and recalling the sound of their laughter, the way her mother would tuck her in at night, and the warmth of her father's reassuring embrace.

"Mom, Dad, I promise I'll make you proud," she would whisper to the empty room, tears streaming down her cheeks. "I'll take care of Aanya. I'll give her everything you wanted for us."

One night, as she finished her work and prepared to head to bed, Aanya peeked into the kitchen. "Are you okay, Sneha?" she asked, her voice soft and filled with concern.

Sneha turned to her sister, forcing a smile despite the exhaustion that weighed on her. "I'm okay, Aanya. Just trying to make sure we're ready for the future."

Aanya nodded, but her eyes were filled with worry. "I'm scared, Sneha. What if we forget them?"

Sneha knelt down, taking Aanya's hands in hers. "We won't forget them. They will always be in our hearts. Every time we laugh, every time we remember the good times, they're with us. We'll keep their memory alive, I promise."

Aanya's eyes shimmered with tears, and Sneha pulled her into a tight embrace. In that moment, Sneha felt a surge of courage. She realized that while they had lost their parents, they still had each other. Together, they could forge a new path, one that honored the love and lessons their parents had given them.

As the days turned into weeks, Sneha began to find strength in the routine they had created. She enrolled

Aanya in school, ensuring that her sister would continue to learn and grow. Each morning, Sneha would walk her to the bus stop, holding her hand tightly, reminding her that they were in this together.

On weekends, they would visit their parents' favorite park, a place filled with memories of laughter and joy. They would sit on the swings, letting the gentle breeze carry away their worries, if only for a moment. "Look, Aanya," Sneha would say, pointing to the sky. "The clouds look like Mom and Dad watching over us."

Aanya would giggle, her eyes lighting up with hope. "Do you think they're happy?"

"I know they are," Sneha replied, her heart swelling with love. "They would be proud of us for being brave."

With each passing day, Sneha felt a shift within herself. The grief that had once consumed her began to transform into a fierce determination to honor her parents' legacy. She was not just surviving; she was learning to thrive, to embrace life with all its challenges and joys.

One evening, as they sat together on the couch, Aanya turned to her with a serious expression. "Sneha, can we do something special for Mom and Dad? Like a party?"

Sneha smiled, her heart warming at the thought. "That's a wonderful idea, Aanya. We can celebrate their lives, all the love they gave us."

And so, they began to plan a small gathering, inviting close friends and family who truly cared for them. They decorated the living room with photos of their parents, lighting candles, and sharing stories that brought laughter and tears. As they celebrated, Sneha felt a sense of peace wash over her.

In that moment, surrounded by love and laughter, she realized that while their parents were no longer physically present, their spirit lived on in every cherished memory, in every act of kindness they shared, and in the bond that had been forged through grief.

As the night drew to a close, Sneha looked around at the faces of those who had come to support them. She felt a renewed sense of purpose. They were not alone. They had each other, and they had a community that cared.

With a heart full of hope, she whispered a silent promise to her parents: "We will keep going. We will live our lives fully, just as you would have wanted. We will make you proud."

And in that moment, Sneha knew that they would rise from the ashes of their loss, stronger and more resilient than ever.

CHAPTER FIVE

Together, Forever

As the seasons changed, so did the landscape of Sneha and Aanya's lives. The initial shock of loss began to settle into a profound understanding of their new reality. They were no longer just two little girls mourning their parents; they were warriors, fighting to keep their memories alive and to build a future that would make their parents proud.

Sneha embraced her role as Aanya's guardian with a fierce determination. Each day, she woke up with a renewed sense of purpose, reminding herself of the promises she had made. She was not just a sister; she was a mother, a father, and a protector. She took charge of their lives, balancing school, work, and the responsibilities of running a household.

Aanya, in turn, blossomed under Sneha's care. The little girl who had once been engulfed in fear and sadness began to shine again. Sneha made sure to nurture Aanya's spirit, encouraging her to explore her interests and passions. They spent evenings painting together, laughing over silly stories, and sharing their dreams. Sneha would often say, "We are a team, Aanya. We can conquer anything together."

Their bond deepened with each passing day. Sneha learned to read Aanya's moods, to recognize when her sister needed comfort or when she simply wanted to play.

They became each other's haven, a sanctuary from the world outside that often felt overwhelming. Sneha would often remind Aanya, "No matter what happens, we have each other. That's what matters most."

As Aanya thrived in school, Sneha felt a swell of pride. She watched her sister make friends, participate in school activities, and even take the stage in a school play. Sneha was always there, cheering her on, her heart bursting with joy. "You were amazing, Aanya!" she would exclaim, enveloping her sister in a warm embrace after every performance.

But it wasn't just Aanya who was growing. Sneha found herself evolving, too. The grief that had once threatened to consume her transformed into a source of strength. She began volunteering at local community centers, sharing her story and helping others who had faced similar losses. She realized that in sharing their journey, she could inspire hope in others.

One evening, as they sat together in their cozy living room, Aanya looked up at Sneha with wide, curious eyes. "Sneha, do you think Mom and Dad would be proud of us?"

In that moment, Sneha felt a rush of emotion. She pulled Aanya close, her heart swelling with love. "I know they are, Aanya. Every day, we honor them by being strong and loving each other. We're living the life they dreamed for us."

Aanya smiled, her innocence a balm for Sneha's soul. "I want to be just like you when I grow up," she said, her voice filled with admiration.

Sneha's heart ached with the weight of that statement. "You can be anything you want, Aanya. Just remember, I'll always be here for you, cheering you on."

As time passed, the sisters created new traditions to celebrate their parents' memory. On special occasions, they would bake their mother's favorite recipes, filling the house with the delicious scents that once danced in the air. They would light candles and share stories about their parents, laughing and crying together as they remembered all the love that had filled their home.

Each moment they shared became a thread in the tapestry of their lives, weaving together the past and the present. They learned to find joy in the little things—a sunset, a shared meal, or a quiet moment together. They understood that while their parents were gone, their love would never fade. It lived on in every smile, every laugh, and every tear they shed together.

One particularly poignant evening, as they sat on the porch watching the sun dip below the horizon, Aanya turned to Sneha with a serious expression. "Sneha, do you ever feel sad? Like really sad?"

Sneha took a deep breath, feeling the weight of her sister's question. "Yes, Aanya. Sometimes I do. But I also feel grateful. Grateful for the time we had with them, for the love they gave us. It's okay to feel sad, but we have to remember the good times too."

Aanya nodded, her eyes glistening with understanding. "I miss them, but I love you so much, Sneha."

"I love you too, Aanya," Sneha replied, her voice thick with emotion. "And I promise, no matter what happens, we'll always be together. We'll face everything together, just like we promised."

As they embraced, Sneha felt a sense of peace wash over her. They were forging a new path, one built on love, resilience, and hope. Together, they were transforming their grief into a powerful force that propelled them forward.

Years passed, and the sisters grew stronger, each step forward a testament to their unbreakable bond. Sneha graduated from college, her hard work and determination paying off. She had pursued her education with the same fervor her parents had instilled in her, driven by the desire to create a brighter future for them both.

Aanya, inspired by her sister's strength, excelled in school, her creativity shining through in every project she undertook. She began to dream of becoming an artist, wanting to share her vision of the world with others. Sneha encouraged her every step of the way, ensuring that Aanya had the tools and support to chase her dreams.

On the day of Sneha's graduation, Aanya stood in the audience, beaming with pride. As Sneha walked across the stage to receive her diploma, she felt her heart swell with gratitude. She had done it—not just for herself, but for Aanya and their parents.

After the ceremony, as they embraced, Aanya looked up at her sister with shining eyes. "You did it, Sneha! I'm so proud of you!"

Sneha knelt down, her heart overflowing with love. "We did it, Aanya. This is just the beginning. We're going to create a beautiful life together, just like Mom and Dad wanted for us."

In that moment, Sneha realized that they had not just survived; they had thrived. They had transformed their pain into purpose, their grief into gratitude. They had become each other's guardians, navigating the world hand in hand, forever bound by the love that had shaped them.

As they stood together, looking toward the future, Sneha felt a sense of hope wash over her. They were not just sisters; they were a force of nature, resilient and unstoppable. Together, they would continue to honor their parents' legacy, carrying their love forward into every new chapter of their lives.

With hearts full of courage and strength, they stepped into the future, ready to embrace whatever came next. The journey ahead would not always be easy, but they knew that as long as they had each other, they could face anything.

As they settled into their new routine, they often spoke to their parents in quiet moments. "We miss you every day," Sneha would whisper, her voice filled with love. "Thank you for teaching us to be strong. We will make you proud." And Aanya would add softly, "We're living our dreams for you, Mom and Dad. Your love guides us always."

And so, with promises kept and dreams ignited, Sneha and Aanya embarked on their next adventure, hand in hand, forever together, forever strong.

"a Cup Of Tea We Never Finished"

From Sneha to her parents

The last words hung in the evening air,
A simple tea, a silent prayer.
"Take care of each other," you gently said,
Smiling above your cups of red.
No goodbye, no final call,
Just warmth and laughter — that was all.
Now every hug I give to her
Feels like your love, quiet and sure.
The tea went cold. The light grew thin,
But you still live beneath my skin.
In every tear, in every song,
You are the place I still belong.

"i Still Hear Her Sing"

From Aanya, remembering Sneha, her protector
She was my compass, loud and bright,
My moon on cold, unbearable nights.
Sneha with eyes like rising suns,
Who taught me that fear can be outrun?
When the world collapsed around our feet,
She wrapped me close in steady heat.
No cape, no magic, no guiding hand
Just her, deciding we'd still stand.
She learned to cook, to fill out the forms,
To hold her own in every storm.
But in the quiet, when no one sees,
She still breaks like the wind in trees.
I watch her smile, but I know the cost,
Of all we found and all we lost.
Still, every night, when silence stings,
I close my eyes, and I hear her sing.
So if you ask what made me grow,
It wasn't time. It wasn't hope.
It was her, my sister, my morning bell,
The girl who walked me out of hell.

Author's Closing Notes

Dear Reader,

Thank you for walking with Sneha and Aanya through the pages of their pain, strength, and unbreakable bond. This story is more than fiction; it is a tribute. Though this story is set around the real-life Pahalgam attack, all characters and events in this book are fictional. This is a tribute to the emotions, the losses, and the silent strength of those who survive the unimaginable.

Loss leaves an empty chair, an unfinished cup of tea, and countless unsaid words. But even in silence, love finds a way to speak. I hope this book helped you feel that.

Let this story be a reminder: even when life shatters around us, the human spirit finds a way to rebuild — with courage, care, and a fierce heart.

To every survivor, every grieving soul, and every quiet fighter, this is for you.

With deepest respect,
Manda Sahithi Sree

About The Author

Manda Sahithi Sree is a passionate storyteller, classical Carnatic music Scholar, and a student of BBA LLB from the Telugu states. Deeply connected to art, emotions, and real-life experiences, she believes that words have the power to heal, inspire, and bring people together.

Apart from her love for writing, Sahithi dedicates her time to teaching and learn music, helping others express themselves through sound and soul. Her stories often reflect strength, lifestyle, silence, sisterhood, and survival, themes close to her heart.

A Cup of Tea We Never Finished is her heartfelt tribute to all the people who have faced sudden tragedy, yet continue to live with love, light, and courage.

This is her debut book. A story that reminds readers that even in the middle of heartbreak, hope can bloom.